Cambridge Early Years

Communication and Language

for English as a First Language

Learner's Book 3C

Gill Budgell

Contents

Note to parents and practitioners — 3

Block 5: How things work — 4

Block 6: Space and the future — 20

Acknowledgements — 32

Note to parents and practitioners

This Learner's Book provides activities to support the third term of FLE Communication and Language for Cambridge Early Years 3.

Activities can be used at school or at home. Children will need support from an adult. Additional guidance about activities can be found in the **For practitioners** boxes.

Stories are provided for children to enjoy looking at and listening to. Children are not expected to be able to read the stories themselves.

Children will encounter the following characters within this book. You could ask children to point to the characters when they see them on the pages, and say their names.

The Learner's Book activities support the Teaching Resource activities. The Teaching Resource provides step-by-step coverage of the Cambridge Early Years curriculum and guidance on how the Learner's Book activities develop the curriculum learning statements.

Hi, my name is Mia.

Find us on the front covers doing lots of fun activities.

Hi, my name is Gemi.

Hi, my name is Rafi.

Hi, my name is Kiho.

Block 5 How things work

Over in the Jungle by Marianne Berkes

Over in the jungle
Where the trees greet the sun
Lived a mother marmoset
And her marmoset **one**.

"Swing," said the mother.
"I swing," said the **one**.
So they swung and they hung
Where the trees greet the sun.

Over in the jungle
Wearing wings of shiny blue
Lived a morpho butterfly
And her little morphos **two**.

"Flit," said the mother.
"We flit," said the **two**.
So they flitted and they fluttered
Wearing wings of shiny blue.

Over in the jungle
On a leafy canopy
Lived a noisy mother parrot
And her little parrots **three**.

"Squawk," said the mother.
"We squawk," said the **three**.
So they squawked and they walked
On a leafy canopy.

Over in the jungle
On a rainforest floor
Lived a leaf cutter ant
And her little ants **four**.

"Scurry," said the mother.
"We scurry," said the **four**.
So they scurried and they hurried
On a rainforest floor.

Over in the jungle
Near a big bee hive
Lived a mother honey bear
And her little honeys **five**.

"Scramble," said the mother.
"We scramble," said the **five**.
So they scrambled and they rambled
Toward a big bee hive.

Over in the jungle
Curled around some mossy sticks
Lived a long mother boa
And her little boas **six**.

"Squeeze," said the mother.
"We squeeze," said the **six**.
So they squeezed and were pleased
Curled around some mossy sticks.

Over in the jungle
In bromeliad heaven
Lived a poison dart frog
And her little froggies **seven**.

"Hop," said the mother.
"We hop," said the **seven**.
So they hopped and they plopped
In bromeliad heaven.

Over in the jungle
Where she knew how to wait
Lived a mother ocelot
And her ocelots **eight**.

"Pounce," said the mother.
"We pounce," said the **eight**.
So they pounced and they bounced
And they learned how to wait.

Over in the jungle
Hanging from a heavy vine
Lived a super-slow sloth
And her little sloths **nine**.

"Creep," said the mother.
"We creep," said the **nine**.
So they crept and they slept,
Hanging from a heavy vine.

Over in the jungle
In their rainforest den
Lived a father howler monkey
And his little howlers **ten**.

"Hoot," said the father.
"We hoot," said the **ten**.
So they hooted and they hollered
In their rainforest den

Over in the jungle, come on, let's take a peek!
In the busy rainforest they're playing hide and seek.
"Find us," say the children. "From **ten** to **one**."
When you find all the creatures then this rhyme is done.

Animal hide and seek

Point and say.

Find the jungle animals in the picture.
Say their names.

Animals in the jungle

For practitioners

Encourage children to explore the picture to find and name each jungle animal.
Prompt them to use language to develop their learning, e.g., to describe or to ask questions.

We're Going into the Jungle

We're going into the jungle. We're going into the jungle.
We're not scared! We're not scared!

Uh-oh! Lions! Big, hairy, ROARING LIONS!

Uh-oh! Monkeys! Jumping, dancing, LAUGHING MONKEYS!

Uh-oh! Crocodiles! Snippy, snappy, SNIPPY-SNAPPY CROCODILES!

Let's run!

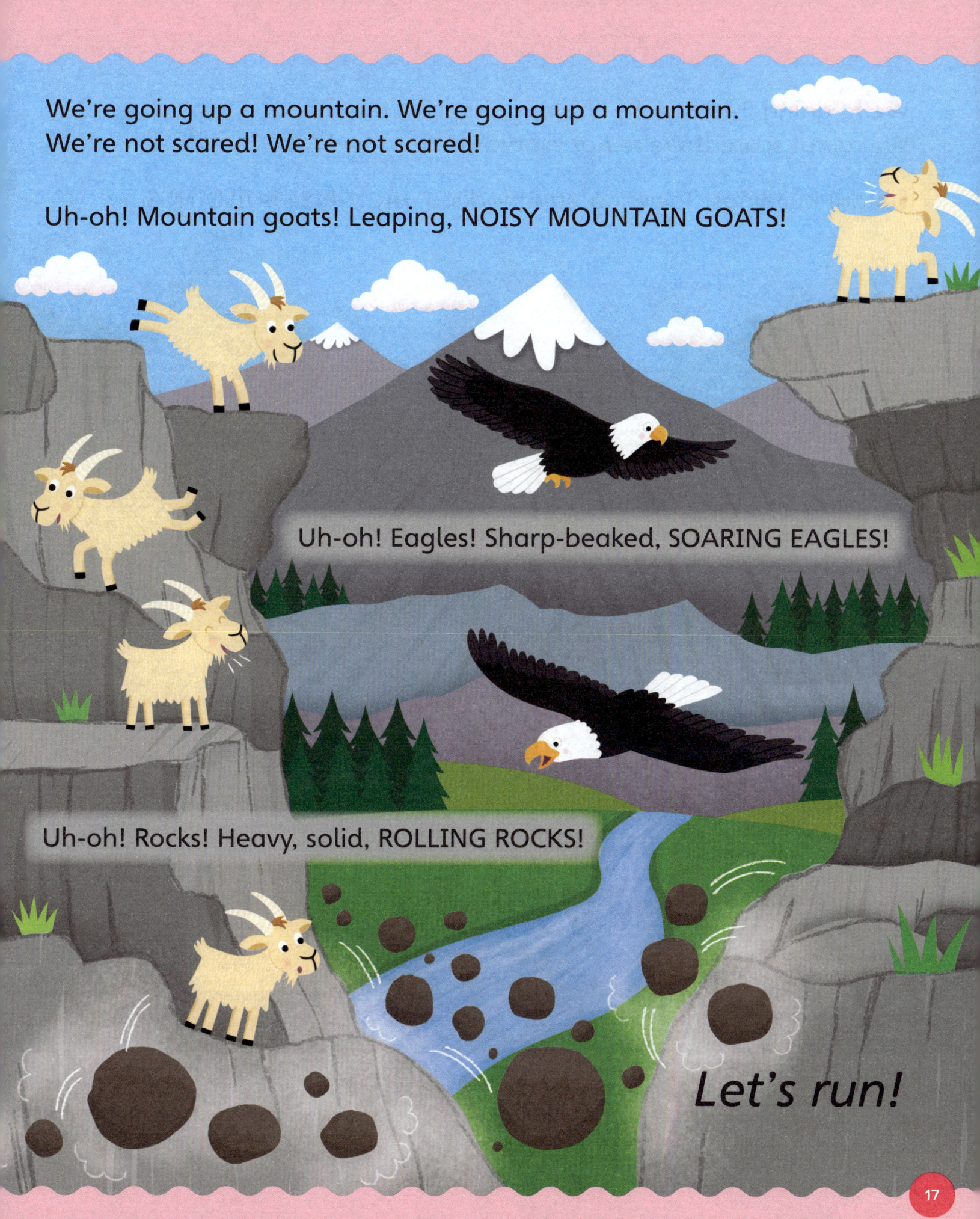

We're going into the city. We're going into the city.
We're not scared! We're not scared!

Uh-oh! Buildings! Towering, sun-blocking, HIGH-RISE BUILDINGS!

Uh-oh! People! Busy, bustling, SCUTTLING PEOPLE!

Uh-oh! Traffic! Beeping, honking, NOISY TRAFFIC!

Let's run!

We're going up a mountain

Think and write.

Draw and write what you see that makes you run!

Uh-oh!
Mountain goats!
Leaping, NOISY
MOUNTAIN GOATS!
Let's run!

Uh-oh!

_____!

_____!

Let's run!

For practitioners
Encourage children to imagine what they might see up a mountain. Support them to record their ideas in writing or pictures as appropriate.

Block 6 Space and the future

Astro Girl
by Ken Wilson-Max

Astrid had loved the stars and space ever since she could remember.

"I want to be an astronaut!"
Astrid said at breakfast.

"Are you sure?" Papa asked. "You'll have to go round and round the Earth in your spaceship."

He swung her around.
"I can do that," Astrid giggled.

"What about eating food out of a tube or a packet every day?"

"I can do that," said Astrid, munching a cereal bar.

"What about all the science experiments?" asked Papa.
"Could you do those, my star princess?"

"Easy-peasy!" said Astrid, as they made her favourite cookies.

At last it was the day they were going to fetch Mama in the car.
Astrid wore her favourite space T-shirt.

At the airbase, they moved to the front of the crowd just in time for the doors to open.

Out walked three people.

"Mama!" shouted Astrid. They hugged and she gave her mum a big kiss.
"Mama, I missed you!
I want to be an astronaut, just like you.
You're my hero."

What do they want to be?

Match and say.

Look at each T-shirt.
Match it to what the children want to be.

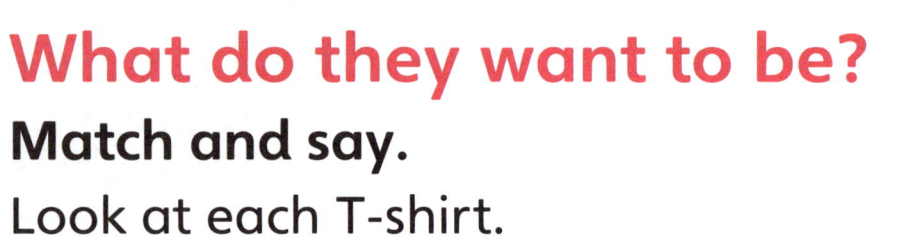
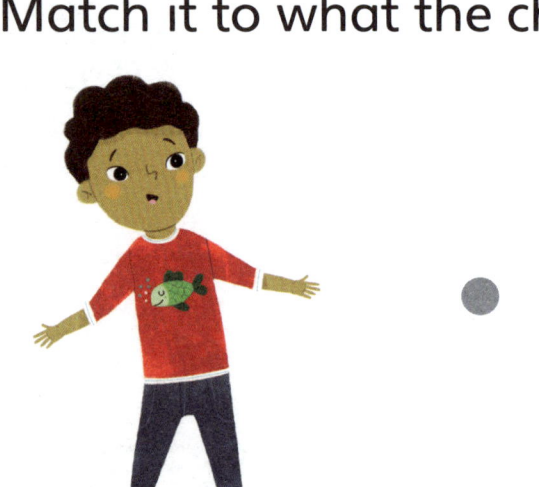

doctor

fisherman

jockey

ballet dancer

astronaut

footballer

For practitioners
Children match each child to the picture of what they want to be when they grow up. Encourage talk to express and clarify their own ideas.

My favourite T-shirt

Read and draw.

Read the sentence.
Then draw what is on your favourite T-shirt.

Astrid wore her favourite space T-shirt.

> **For practitioners**
> Children read the sentence and draw what is on their own favourite T-shirt.
> Some children may want to write their own sentence with support.

Immediate Despatch by Jean Gilbert

Polish up the spaceship,
Shine, shine, shine,
Fill up the fuel tanks
In time, time, time.
Switch on the motor
And close down the hatch.
Moonship Apollo
Immediate despatch.

Shooting into outer space
Zoom, zoom, zoom,
Circling round and round the Earth
There's room, room, room,
Watch every lever
And check every clock.
Moonship Apollo
Is ready to dock.

Fill the gaps

Trace and write.

Say the rhyme. Trace the grey word and write it again.

Polish up the spaceship,

Shine, shine, _____.

Fill up the fuel tanks

In time, time, _____.

For practitioners
Read the words together and encourage the children to recognise the repetition of the final word. They trace it and attempt to write it.

Make a Moonship Apollo

Draw.

Draw your own Moonship Apollo.

For practitioners
As children work, encourage them to talk about their choices and ideas.

Acknowledgements

The authors and publishers acknowledge the following sources of copyright material and are grateful for the permissions granted. While every effort has been made, it has not always been possible to identify the sources of all the material used, or to trace all copyright holders. If any omissions are brought to our notice, we will be happy to include the appropriate acknowledgements on reprinting.

Over in the Jungle by Marianne Berkes, illustrated by Jeanette Canyon, published by Dawn Publications. © 2007 Marianne Berkes, illustration © 2007 Jeanette Canyon.

Material from *Astro Girl* by Ken Wilson-Max, used by permission of Otter-Barry Books Ltd.

'Immediate Despatch' attributed to Jean Gilbert in *Topic Anthology*, Oxford University Press, 1980, believed to be adapted from 'Immediate Despatch' by Elizabeth Horscroft in *Space Songs for Infants*, Edwin Ashdown Ltd, 1971. Illustration on page 29 & 30 by A-Y-N/Getty Images

Thanks to the following artists at Beehive Illustration:
Lays Bittencourt, Veronika Chaves, Joe Wilkins.

Cover characters by Becky Davies (The Bright Agency)